This igloo book belongs to:

....

ACCESS ALL AREAS

ADMIT ONE

igloobooks

Published in 2021
First published in the UK by Igloo Books Ltd
An imprint of Igloo Books Ltd
Cottage Farm, NN6 0BJ, UK
Owned by Bonnier Books
Sveavägen 56, Stockholm, Sweden
www.igloobooks.com

0921 002
2 4 6 8 10 9 7 5 3
ISBN 978-1-80022-446-9

Written by Claire Mowat
Illustrated by Leire Martín

Designed by Jason Shortland
Edited by Claire Mowat

Printed and manufactured in China

THE
STAR
OF THE
SHOW

igloobooks

The talented animals all *dance* and *sing*.
Their exciting new show is just missing one thing.

They need to decide who will **star** in the show.

So, Unicorn stands up and she says, "I know!"

She says, "Just look at me. I'm the perfect star!"

I'm *magic*...

... I'm *awesome*...

... I'm the *best* by far!"

Pug says, "I'm sorry, I think that you're wrong.
I know someone else who can sing a great song!"

"I can," says Pug. "I'm so **small** and so *cute.*
I look super sweet when I sing in my suit."

"Hmm," Llama says. "I'm not sure that you're right.
Someone else here is made for the **spotlight.**"

La,

La,

... sings Llama in her pretty gown.
"I'll be fantastic. I won't let you down."

Sloth joins in too and, as usual, he's yawning.
"It should be me," he says. "I'm never **boring!**"

Sloth says, "I'd be a great **star** of the show!
My fans will all want seats right on the front row."

"You're too slow," Giraffe says, "and you're much too small. The star needs to be someone that's **really tall!**"

Giraffe says, "I should be the top of the list!
Pick me! I'm so tall that I just can't be missed."

"No!" the friends shout. "That main part is all ***mine!***"
They argue and sulk, for they each want to shine.

Their squabbling stops when
they hear a sweet sound.

"Who **is** that?" they ask
as they all look around.

They really have **no idea** who it could be.
So, they follow the noise and who do they see?

It's **Goldfish!** He's singing backstage in his bowl!
Pug grins. "I know who should play the lead role."
Finally, everyone's glad to agree.
There's only one animal their **star** can be!

"Goldie," says Sloth, "you have such a great voice.
Be our big star. You are the **perfect choice!**"

"Me?" Goldie says. "But I'm just a small fish.
Though singing on stage really is my great wish!"

The show is a hit and the crowd cheers. **_Woo-hoo!_**
Goldie's a huge star. His friends all are, too.

"It wasn't just me," he says. "This stage is ours.
Together, we have a whole show of great stars."

"*The superstar singing sensation*"

Goldie

"*The best show I have ever seen!*"

"*Six stars!*"

Unicorn

Pug

Llama

Sloth

Giraffe